Children's Books:

The Monkey Who Couldn't Make Up His Mind

Sally Huss

ISBN: 0692651934
ISBN 13: 9780692651933

A very hungry monkey swings down from the trees

To explore a rustic, jungle resort that he sees.

Hungry as he is, he goes straight to the dining room
with its buffet table…

And gets in line as best as he is able.

He reads the sign over the small plates stacked near the food.

"Pick one item only," it reads.

He thinks… this will be a challenge, but I'll do what I should.

After taking a plate, the monkey looks
at the bowl of apples before him.

An apple is delicious, nutritious, and fine.

It is filled with such sweetness that I consider quite divine.

As he places an apple on his plate,

He looks at the next bowl and changes his fate.

It is filled with pear upon pear.

Then he thinks… if I don't have an apple,

I could have a pear.

A pear is rare in its fragrance and taste.

I could eat the whole thing without leaving a trace.

With that, he switches the apple for the pear,

And then looks around to see what else is there.

His eye spots a platter of bananas.

He thinks… if I don't have a pear, I could have a banana.

Oh my, oh my, bananas are my favorite food.

The truth is I'm always in a banana mood.

He puts the pear back and takes one banana from the bunch.

He knows it will make a very tasty lunch.

Just then his eye catches a bowl of grapes.

He reasons… if I don't have a banana,

I could have some grapes.

Grapes are gorgeous, moist, and sugary,

Just the ticket for one so hungry.

Grapes -- big, plump, purple grapes

Are better than a stack of cakes.

Perhaps he should try a stem or two.

Back goes the banana and on his plate he puts a few.

Then as he moves along the buffet line,

He sees something else he thinks is fine – tomatoes.

If I don't have the grapes, he thinks, I could have a tomato.

One cute tomato does not a salad make,

But a single tomato without a salad is perfect and that's what I'll take.

So the tomato bumps the grapes back to their original bowl

While along the line the monkey continues to stroll.

He is happy with his tomato until he sees what is next
— a basket of avocados. Now, he is truly perplexed.

Oh yes, an avocado is the most exotic of all fruit.

You can eat it plain, on a salad, or in soup.

If I don't have the tomato, he thinks,

I could have an avocado.

He is still trying to figure out whether he shouldn't

or whether he ought to…

When in a daring move, without the slightest hitch,

With his arm flailing, he makes the switch.

He moves the tomato back to its place

And places the avocado on his plate's space.

His taste buds are watering. His stomach is hollering,

but his eyes are still wandering.

What they land on now is a platter of corn

that is wallowing.

Corn with melted butter is so luscious and yellow.

And when I eat it, I feel so delightfully mellow.

If I don't have the avocado, he ponders,

I could have the corn.

So the avocado goes the way of the tomato,

back to the table…

And the corn very quickly itself becomes unstable

Because the monkey now sees a grand baked potato.

If I don't have the corn, he reasons, I could have a potato.

Oh, a potato is one vegetable that is grown in the ground,

No better nourishment can hardly be found.

After picking the potato, the monkey finds himself

at the end of the line.

"There is no going back," he reads on the sign.

The monkey looks at his plain, brown potato and thinks about

all the glorious food he could have had.

This makes him more than a little bit sad.

The monkey, still hungry and with quite a thirst,

Says, "I wish I had a juicy apple. It's what I picked first.

In the future, I'll make better choices

when the choices are up to me

And not be so swayed by what I next see."

With that, a kind waiter, who is standing nearby,

Could see that the monkey was about to cry.

Quickly, he moves down the line of the buffet,

Reaches in and takes an apple away.

He places it on the monkey's dish,

Happily fulfilling the monkey's wish.

"Next time," declares the monkey, "when choosing

between that and this

I'll make sure that what I already have

isn't something I won't miss."

The end,
but not the end
of making
good choices.

At the end of this book you will find a Certificate of Merit that may be issued to any child who has fulfilled the requirements stated in the Certificate. This fine Certificate will easily fit into a 5"x7" frame, and happily suit any girl or boy who receives it!

Sally writes new books all the time. If you would like to be alerted when one of her new books becomes available or when one of her books is offered FREE on Amazon, sign up here: http://www.sallyhuss.com/kids-books.html.

If you liked *The Monkey Who Couldn't Make Up His Mind*, please be kind enough to post a short review on Amazon. Here is the link: http://amzn.com/B01C26KV58.

Here are a few Sally Huss books you might enjoy. They may be found on Amazon as e-books or in soft cover.

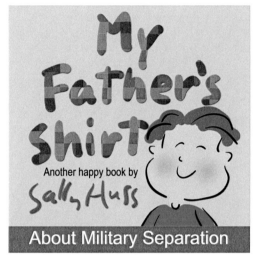

http://amzn.com/B018JQP8So

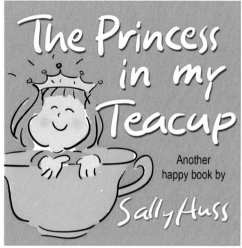

http://amzn.com/B00NG4EDH8

http://amzn.com/B0125714B4

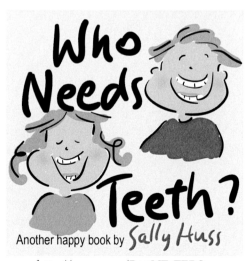

http://amzn.com/B00MT5TERO

About the Author/Illustrator

Sally Huss

"Bright and happy," "light and whimsical" have been the catch phrases attached to the writings and art of Sally Huss for over 30 years. Sweet images dance across all of Sally's creations, whether in the form of children's books, paintings, wallpaper, ceramics, baby bibs, purses, clothing, or her King Features syndicated newspaper panel "Happy Musings."

Sally creates children's books to uplift the lives of children and hopes you will join her in this effort by helping spread her happy messages.

Sally is a graduate of USC with a degree in Fine Art and through the years has had 26 of her own licensed art galleries throughout the world.

This certificate may be cut out, framed, and presented to any child who has earned it.

Certificate of Merit

(Name)

The child named above is awarded this Certificate of Merit for:
*Making good choices
*Appreciating what he or she has
*Being grateful for the kindness of others

Presented by: _____

Date: _____

44123701R00025

Made in the USA
Middletown, DE
28 May 2017